WHAT HAPPENED

SANDWICH
SHENANIGANS

Book design by Jake Slavik
Illustrations by Courtney Huddleston

Design Elements: Shutterstock Images

Published in the United States by Jolly Fish Press, an imprint of North Star Editions, Inc.

First Edition
First Printing, 2019

This is a work of fiction. Names, characters, places, and incidents are either the product of the author's imagination or are used fictitiously, and any resemblance to actual persons living or dead, business establishments, events, or locales is entirely coincidental.

Library of Congress Cataloging-in-Publication Data
Names: Weaver, Verity, author. | Huddleston, Courtney, illustrator.
Title: Sandwich shenanigans / by Verity Weaver ; illustrated by Courtney Huddleston.
Description: First edition. | Mendota Heights, MN : Jolly Fish Press, [2020] | Summary: "Sam Witt's sandwich—his project for the STEAM Project Fair—is missing, and his classmates all have different theories about what happened to it"—Provided by publisher.
Identifiers: LCCN 2019001863 (print) | LCCN 2019004533 (ebook) | ISBN 9781631633171 (ebook) | ISBN 9781631633164 (pbk.) | ISBN 9781631633157 (hardcover)
Subjects: | CYAC: Lost and found possessions—Fiction. | Sandwiches—Fiction | Science projects—Fiction. | Schools—Fiction. | LCGFT: Fiction.
Classification: LCC PZ7.1.W41777 (ebook) | LCC PZ7.1.W41777 San 2019 (print) | DDC [Fic]—dc23
LC record available at https://lccn.loc.gov/2019001863

Jolly Fish Press
North Star Editions, Inc.
2297 Waters Drive
Mendota Heights, MN 55120
www.jollyfishpress.com

Printed in the United States of America

WHAT HAPPENED?

SANDWICH SHENANIGANS

by VERITY WEAVER

illustrated by COURTNEY HUDDLESTON

text by JENNIFER MOORE

JOLLY
FiSH
PRESS

Mendota Heights, Minnesota

Chapter 1
MISSING

Monday, May 6, 7:48 a.m.

It was Monday morning. Not just any Monday morning, though. Not for Mr. Hargrove's class, staggering into school with still-wet paintings, dioramas, and not-so-miniature Statues of Liberty for the fifth-grade STEAM project fair. Students lugged around home-sewn patchwork quilts, sequined dance costumes, something that looked suspiciously like a stuffed alligator head peering out from under a dishcloth, and no fewer than three Brooklyn Bridges built from craft sticks. The first two bridges made it all the way to class in perfect condition, but the third looked as if it had fought with Godzilla on the way in . . . and lost. Yes, there was a Godzilla too, an enormous snarling one made of papier-mâché, with a wild look in his painted eyes and a bridge-shaped dent at the end of his scaly nose.

"Your project can be anything you want," Mr. Hargrove had told the students a few weeks earlier, "as long as it follows the theme of this term's topic: What My Country Means to Me. You might want to base it on a special place, a special memory, or a special person. It's entirely up to you. And the good news is that Miss Patterson and I will be working on a project of our own as well—a themed treasure hunt around the school on the morning of the fair, as a reward for all your hard work."

It had been hard work, yes, but fun too. And apart from the poor owner of Craft-Stick Bridge Number Three (who'd disappeared into the stationery cupboard in search of some radioactive-monster-proof glue), the students couldn't have been more pleased with the finished results, proudly showing off their own projects while admiring everyone else's.

"Another Brooklyn Bridge? Snap!"

"I've never seen an alligator up close before. Look at those teeth!"

"Ninety-seven verses? That must be the longest poem about a football game EVER!"

There was no shortage of unique ideas. Jake Parry had made a four-hour film about libraries. Mina Henderson had made a tiny model of her own house inside a matchbox. And Sam Witt . . . well, Sam had made a sandwich. That's right, Sam Witt's finished project was a sandwich. But oh boy, what a sandwich it was.

It was a wonder. A whopper. An eye-boggling, breathtaking, jaw-dropper of a thing. It was America on a plate, with flag-topped burger picks to keep the tomatoes from escaping and a different filling for each state. Yes, Sam Witt's sandwich was a work of art—a triple-quadruple decker built with loaf-sized slices and stuffed with some of the most delicious foods known to man; from pastrami, pickles, and peanut butter to chipotle, chicken, and cheese, with sauces in all the colors of the rainbow.

The other projects were forgotten the moment Sam walked in with his creation, his classmates jostling around his desk for a closer look.

"Holy underpants, Batman," said Ravi, eyes bulging behind his steamed-up glasses, "that's INCREDIBLE! It's a mega-mutant monster!"

"I wish I'd thought of this," said Mateo, licking his lips. "It looks delicious."

"That is one eee-norrrr-mous sandwich," announced Deena in her best funny voice. "That sandwich deserves a place in the—" She stopped short, glancing up at the teacher who'd appeared in the doorway. "Who's that?" she whispered. "And where's Mr. Hargrove?"

"Good morning, students," said the teacher in question, heading for Mr. Hargrove's desk. She was a tall lady with a shock of long red hair and a huge, bulging stomach. She was clearly several months pregnant. "My name is Mrs. Ample, and I'll be teaching your class this morning. If you could leave your projects at the back and find your seats, we'll be ready to begin."

"What happened to Mr. Hargrove?" asked Ravi, wiping his glasses on the front of his T-shirt. "He's supposed to be putting on a treasure hunt for us today. A joint one with Miss Patterson's class."

There was a loud chorus of disappointed groans as the students remembered their last substitute teacher, who'd treated them to a two-hour math test—in silence—followed by an hour of spelling.

"Don't worry," Mrs. Ample assured them. "I understand from

Miss Patterson that the treasure hunt is already set up, with more than a hundred fact cards hidden around the school grounds for you to find. Each card covers a different fact about the United States, so you'll be learning as you go. Don't look so anxious," she added. "There's no reason why the hunt can't go ahead as planned once we've taken attendance."

The children's groans turned to cheers, and all thoughts of Mr. Hargrove were forgotten, especially when Mrs. Ample explained that there'd be prizes for the class who found the most cards. This was their class's big chance to beat those boastful show-offs next door! The students ferried their projects to the long table at the back of the room, with Sam Witt's sandwich in pride of place, like a glowing beacon of breaded wonder, then hurried back to their seats for attendance.

"Here."

"Yep."

"Present."

Mrs. Ample ticked them all off one by one (apart from Shaniqua, who would probably be late as usual) and then sent them next door to get their instructions for the treasure hunt. She'd be out to help supervise in a bit, she told them, once she finished getting everything ready for the fair.

WHOOSH!

SCRAM!

CLATTER!

The students didn't need to be told twice. They were off, dashing into the hallway and pushing past one another to get to Miss Patterson's classroom before they missed out on any clues. And there was Shaniqua tearing towards them with a giant collage tucked under her arm, shouting something crazy about an escaped tiger.

"Ha, ha! Good one," said Ravi. "I hope he doesn't eat the fact cards before we find them."

"Don't worry," said Mateo. "I'll knock him out with one of Mom's sugar-free rock buns. They're enough to finish anyone off!" Mateo was always complaining about his mother's unappetizing new recipes.

"This isn't a joke," Shaniqua told them, glancing back over her shoulder. "I'm *serious.*"

"Yeah, right," said Deena. "Just like the time you found a piranha fish in the swimming pool . . . or the time the headmaster got kidnapped by clowns." Shaniqua was known for her active imagination.

"Come on," Sam interrupted. "We don't want them to start without us. Leave your project at the back of the class with the others," he told Shaniqua, who was sticking to her story like glue. "There's a bit of space next to my sandwich. But watch out for the flags. I don't want them getting squashed before the fair this afternoon." And with that he was off, jostling into Miss Patterson's room with the others, anxious to begin.

Squashed flags were the least of Sam's worries, as it turned out. Maybe if he'd known the terrible fate awaiting his poor sandwich he'd have stopped to kiss it goodbye before he left. Maybe even a farewell nibble of stray salami while he straightened the flags one last time.

Because when everyone returned to the classroom, some two hours later, there were no flags left for Sam to straighten. No salami slices making a break for freedom. No delicious fillings of any kind, fighting for space on a bouncy bed of bread. No colorful sauces oozing out of the sides like liquid happiness, because...

SHOCK!

HORROR!

. . . and some high-pitched squeals of disbelief . . .

Sam's sandwich wasn't there anymore.

It wasn't at the back of the class where he'd left it, and it wasn't at the front of the class with Mrs. Ample's cardigan and folder, either. It wasn't on his desk with his Star Wars pencil case, and it wasn't under his desk with the dried mud off his sneakers and an abandoned pile of pencil shavings. It wasn't anywhere. The king of all sandwiches, the cheesy, meaty, salad-y emperor of lunchtime creations had disappeared. Gone. Vanished without a trace.

Nooooooooooooooooooooooooooooooo!

It was true. There wasn't a single crumb left to follow.

No telltale trail of lettuce.

No saucy drips leading out of the classroom.

No clues whatsoever, in fact.

Or *were* there?

Chapter 2

Ravi, 7:49 a.m.

I couldn't wait to show the others my moon landing model. Especially the little green alien peeking out of one of the craters. That was Daada's—my grandad's—suggestion; he's full of good ideas. And it turns out he's also the world's number-one expert at making model aliens out of pipe cleaners. He showed me how to do it last night, while we were watching *Revenge of the Astronomic Overlords* for the nine hundred and forty-seventh time, and once I'd started, I couldn't stop. By the time the evil emperor melted into a pool of toxic, orange gunk (the best part of the whole movie), there was an entire army of pipe-cleaner aliens slithering around the living room, like extra-terrestrial slug-monsters.

SLWOOSH.

BURBLE.

BURP.

Unfortunately, one of them slithered right under Daada's wheelchair and got squished (*Ha! Take that, you pesky slimeball!*), but that still left thirty-three. I wanted to use them *all* on my STEAM project but Daada said that sometimes "less is more." So we decided to save the others for a *War of the Slime Creatures* battle reconstruction next weekend instead. It's going to be pipe-cleaner aliens versus Goo Attack collectibles, with a real Jell-O slime field for them to battle through. How cool is that?

Anyway, back to this morning . . . I was pretty excited about my moon model when I first brought it into school. But once I saw Sam's sandwich, I forgot all about homemade craters and moon dust. I forgot about the monsters and aliens (which doesn't happen very often) and trying to decide on the best flavor Jell-O for a slime field. I forgot about *everything*.

Wowzers! That sandwich was OUT OF THIS WORLD! It had more fillings than a rotten-toothed vampire fish, and a different sauce for every day of the week, oozing out of the sides like mutant slug slime. It was as big as a Martian mushburger (the giant ones from the alien diner in *Return to The Red Planet*) and a squillion times tastier-looking. It was the superhero of the sandwich world, only with capers instead of a cape. *Don't worry, little crusts. I'll save you!*

There wasn't much time to admire it, though, because Mrs. Ample (the substitute teacher) made us leave our projects at the back of the class before we trooped next door to get our final instructions:

Be quiet and respectful of other classes.

No running in the hallways.

No pushing.

No snatching.

NO SURRENDER!!! (I might have made that last one up. That's what they say at the end of *Battle of the Killer Ooze-Heads*, just before the spaceship disappears into the ooze vortex.)

We decided to split up to cover more ground, maximizing our chances of beating Miss Patterson's lot. *She* said it was just a bit of friendly competition between her class and ours, but I could tell by the looks on our enemies' faces that they knew better. This wasn't just a treasure hunt . . . this was a fight to the finish.

I headed straight for the jungle gym on the top field. If I was Mr. Hargrove, I decided, that's where *I'd* hide a fact card. I'd stick it to the inside of the lookout dome, so no one could see it unless they climbed all the way to the top. I wasn't thinking like

Mr. Hargrove for long, though. I was too busy pretending to be Captain Silverpants in *Escape to the Watery Wildlands*, leaping across the backs of imaginary croco-sharks to reach the safety of the jagged rocks.

BOING!

SPLOSH!

SNAP!

Aaaahh, get off me, you toothsome terror. Give me back my leg!

Croco-sharks are the worst. They skulk unseen under the water, their dorsal fins twitching. And all the while they're watching and waiting, stalking passing treasure hunters through unblinking yellow eyes and waiting to pounce. It takes a brave and fearless hero to venture into a croco-shark-infested lagoon. One step too far in the wrong direction and *whoosh!* Suddenly the whole field (I mean, lagoon) is a writhing tangle of snapping jaws and razor teeth; of powerful claws and flicking tails. Your only chance of escape is to reach solid ground before their gills seal up and they switch into land mode. Because once those beasts get a taste for human flesh, there's no stopping them. Unless you're Captain Silverpants, of course.

I wrestled my leg free from the croco-shark's bone-tearing jaws (seeing him off with both barrels of my laser attack stare— *FIZZZZZ! POW!*) and made it to the jagged rocks of the climbing frame. Phew! Now to clamber my way to safety, find the hidden treasure, and make my escape.

The croco-sharks were still snapping at my heels as I scrambled up the bars, their breath hot against the backs of my legs. There were more of them now—hundreds of the creatures swarming toward the rocks, clamoring for a bite of fearless alien sea captain.

SCRATCH!

CHOMP!

CRUNCH!

"Snap all you like, you brutish beasts," I roared in my best Captain's voice. "You'll never take me alive. No one can defeat Captain Silverpants and his intergalactic stink blaster." And with that I reached into my pocket, ready to zap the lot of them, to find it gone. No, I don't mean the stink blaster—that was as imaginary as the croco-sharks. I mean my Goo Attack collectible. The one I'd smuggled into school that morning, despite the recent ban, at the risk of getting it confiscated for THE REST OF THE YEAR.

It wasn't just any old Goo Attack monster, either. It was Sticky Stu Boggle Eyes, the rarest of the lot. I'd snatched him up in a hurry as I was leaving my bedroom, without stopping to check which one it was. And then, when I *did* realize, it was too late to run back and swap him for a less precious one because Mom and Daada were already waiting for me in the car.

I checked my pocket again, more thoroughly this time, hoping against hope that I'd made a mistake. Maybe he was hiding in one of the corners, away from searching fingers. I found a hole—a Goo Attack collectible-sized hole—but no Sticky Stu.

No, no, no, no, no.

My glasses were steaming up with worry as I tried my other pocket. He'd definitely still been there when I got to class because I'd pulled him out by mistake instead of a tissue. The tissue was still there now, together with two sticky candy wrappers (strawberry flavor, I'd guess, judging by the smell of my fingers) but no Sticky Stu. I tried my back pocket—twice—and then when I ran out of pockets, I took off my shoes and shook them out in case he'd slipped down my leg when I wasn't looking. (If you've ever tried taking your shoes off halfway up a climbing frame, you'll know how tricky that is.) But it was no good. He was gone. How could I have been so stupid?

There were no more croco-sharks after that. No more Captain Silverpants. No more racing to find the treasure cards before Miss Patterson's class. I had a brand-new quest now: The Hunt for Sticky Stu Boggle Eyes. I had to find him, I just *had* to. And I needed to do it quickly, before one of the teachers spotted him. Before they locked him up in the principal's Confiscation Cupboard of Doom.

I retraced my steps, desperate for a glimpse of sticky, purple goo peeking out from the forest of grass at my feet. I even got down on my hands and knees and crawled the last bit, to make sure I didn't miss him. But he wasn't on the field, and he wasn't on the playground, either, which meant he must be somewhere inside the school building.

Would I have been in such a hurry to go back in if I'd have known what was waiting for me there? Would I been brave enough to face them on my own? Who knows. What I *do* know is that it wasn't just Sam's sandwich that was out of this world. Not anymore.

Chapter 3

Ravi, 8:50 a.m.

I was super careful at first, creeping along the hallways like a secret spy in *Revenge of the Three-Headed Moon Dog*, in case I ran into any teachers. And then I remembered that I was supposed to be on a treasure hunt, so there was no need to tiptoe around the place. If anyone asked me what I was looking for, I'd tell them it was one of the hidden fact cards.

I shouldn't have worried anyway. The place was oddly deserted, with the teachers closeted away inside their classrooms and no sign of any other kids. I guess they must have searched that section of the building already and moved on. The only other person I spotted was Shaniqua, perched in the library window seat with a heavy-looking book, checking for fact cards between the pages. I felt bad when I saw how seriously she was taking the treasure hunt—I hadn't managed to find a single card yet—but this was an emergency. Sticky Stu needed me.

There was a peculiar, greenish light coming from our classroom as I turned the final corner. It flickered and pulsed through the glass panel in the door, spilling out into the hallway in soft emerald waves. I didn't think much of it at first because I was too busy looking for Stu—too busy worrying that I'd lost him forever. But there he was, lying upside down in a little puddle of juice (looking stickier than ever) just outside Miss Patterson's room. Thank goodness for that. He must have slipped through the hole in my pocket on the way out and been waiting patiently for me to come back and rescue him.

"Holy sweat socks, Batman! Don't ever do that to me again," I told him sternly, scooping him up and checking him over.

Stu, being Stu, said nothing. But he didn't seem too scarred by the experience. His retractable stomach goo was still working fine, and his plastic-molded grin was as wide as ever. Phew!

I wiped the juice off onto my T-shirt and tucked him back

into my pocket for safe-keeping. My *good* pocket, I mean. Not the one with the built-in Goo Attack ejector seat.

"And now to get me some treasure," I announced to the empty hallway, slipping back into my Captain Silverpants voice. "Time to show those rascally rivals in Miss Patterson's class who the best fifth grade . . . Wait a minute. What *is* that?"

With Sticky Stu safe and sound in my pocket, I turned my attention to the green light spilling out of Mr. Hargrove's room. It reminded me of the opening scene in *They Came from the Planet Zing*, when the leader of the Anti-Extra-Terrestrial Task Force spots a pulsing green light in the sky where the sun's supposed to be. That's when the spooky electronic music creeps in and the strange silver disks start to materialize out of nowhere. Daada and I must have watched that film at least twenty times, but that first scene still sends shivers down my spine.

Uh-oh. My spine was shivering like mad just thinking about the hideous two-headed creatures in the movie, spilling out of the silver spaceships like an unstoppable army. And it wasn't only my spine, either. My legs were a shivering, quivering mess of Jell-O as I crept along the hallway, hardly daring to breathe. And as for my stomach, it wasn't a case of a few nervous butterflies fluttering in my tummy. It was a full-on wiggling, wriggling ball of squirming snakes, like a heaving nest of zombie vipers twisting around my guts.

I'd imagined this moment so many times before—the moment when aliens first arrived on Earth—and now it was actually here. This wasn't a film, though, I realized. Not this time. And that wasn't a special effect flickering through the darkness of the classroom as I pressed my trembling face to the glass. This was real life. Those were real alien plasma beams pulsing in the gloom. And the gruesome space monster rearing up out of nowhere was as real as the sweat pooling on my upper lip.

"Holy Swiss chee—" The words died on my tongue as I counted the heads in the doorway. *One. Two . . .*

I didn't need an Anti-Extra-Terrestrial Task Force badge to know that two heads were BAD NEWS. Like SERIOUSLY BAD NEWS. Yes, two heads might be better than one when it comes to solving a tricky problem. And two heads are definitely better than one for planning a pipe-cleaner aliens versus Goo Attack collectibles *War of the Slime Creatures* battle reconstruction. But when it comes to creepy monster shadows seen through the door of your own classroom, two heads are A MILLION times worse than one.

If it was just the one head, I might have gotten away with a swallowed gulp of fear or a high-pitched squeal of terrified surprise. But two heads turned it into a full-on scream scenario—a lung-bursting, eardrum-splitting solid wall of noise:

"AAAAAAAAGGGGGGGGGHHHHHHHHH!!!"

It's funny, I always thought I'd be superhero brave and daring when I met my first evil alien invader. I imagined myself laughing in the face of danger and karate-chopping them into slimy little pieces with my bare hands. *Take that, you miserable maggots. No one invades* my *planet and gets away with it.*

OOF!

POW!

KERSPLAT!

But it turns out I wasn't such a superhero after all. I didn't want to save the world single-handedly from their oozing overlords. I didn't want to risk my life battling bone-melting blubber-creatures from another galaxy. I just wanted to scream.

"AAAAAAAAGGGGGGGGGHHHHHHHHH!!!"

And after that, I wanted to run. In fact, what I *really* wanted was to do both together—scream *and* run. The perfect combination.

Chapter 4

Ravi, 9:00 a.m.

"AAAAAAAAGGGGGGGGHHHHHHHH!!!"

COUGH!

SPLUTTER!

GASP!

Holy pasta strainers, Batman! Screaming and running at the same time was SO much harder than it looked. I was panting and wheezing like a pig with a blocked nose by the time I reached the boys' bathroom. Then I remembered what Miss Patterson said about not running in the hallways, and I skidded to a halt. Did the same rule apply to two-headed intergalactic monsters too? Or should that be "no sliming in the hallways?" I braved a shaky glance over my shoulder, expecting to see an entire army of hideous, rule-breaking creatures sliming after me, but the hallway was empty. For now, anyway. Phew.

And what was the other thing Miss Patterson said? (It seemed a world away now). Oh yes, "be quiet and respectful of other classes." That was it. I guessed that meant no screaming, either, which was just as well really—it was giving me a sore throat and making me an easy target for the monsters to track. I decided to trade noisy running for quietly keeping out of the aliens' way, and to swap screaming like a runaway firework for hiding like a hibernating hedgehog. That seemed like a *much* better plan.

"D-d-don't worry," I whispered to Sticky Stu Boggle Eyes, giving him a reassuring squeeze inside my pocket. "I know the p-perfect place."

For the record, I wasn't hiding from aliens because I was a weak Earthling scaredy-cat—that wasn't the reason at all. I was just getting over the shock of it all. Just getting my strength back so I could save the world from a gruesome, gooey fate. That's what the boy hero does in *They Came from the Planet Zing*—he hides out in an abandoned dentist's office while everyone else is getting alien-goo gunked. Then *SPLAT! SLAM! SUPER-SQUIRT!*

Out he comes with the biggest tube of toothpaste on the planet and minty-freshens the monsters into a melted blubber bath. It turns out they're allergic to clean teeth! Or maybe it's the mint they don't like. Either way, the rest of the aliens return to their flying saucers and zip back to the planet Zing never to be seen again, and the hero gets a medal from the President of the United States. And then everyone brushes their teeth extra carefully for the rest of the film.

I ducked into the boys' bathroom. There wasn't any toothpaste in there, unfortunately, but there *was* soap. I could always try foaming them into melted blubber if they got too close. That would teach them! Or maybe the general smell of the place would be enough to put off any passing aliens until reinforcements arrived. It *was* pretty stinky in there.

Toby Fishwick, from Miss Patterson's class, was coming out the door as I went in. He gave me a funny look—half embarrassed, half curious—but dashed off down the hallway before I could get enough breath back to warn him. He probably wanted to get to the next treasure hunt fact card before me, as if the treasure hunt still mattered with the future of the entire planet hanging in the balance.

"W-w-w-watch . . . out . . . for . . . t-t-two-headed slime monsters," I called after him, but it was too late. He was gone. He probably wouldn't have believed me anyway. That's how it works in the old invasion movies Daada and I watch—no one ever believes the guy who first spots the aliens. Not until it's too late.

At least Toby was headed *away* from Mr. Hargrove's class. Away from the pulsing green light and that hideous, two-headed shadow. He was also the fastest boy in the fifth grade, so he'd be able to outrun a lumbering slime monster easily. That's what I told myself as I collapsed, panting, against the nearest sink, my glasses steaming up all over again with the delayed shock of it all. Real-life aliens right here in my school! In my own classroom!

That's when I heard it. A horrible snuffling sound outside the bathroom door. A sniffling, snuffling, shuffling noise getting closer and closer. *YIKES!* My knees were knocking like castanets as I filled my hands with soap, ready to launch a bubble attack on the blubbery creature the moment his double heads appeared around the door.

You can do this, I told myself, thinking about the medal I'd get from the President when he heard about my daring battle. Thinking how proud Daada would be when he saw my face flash up on the news that night: *Brave Schoolboy Hero Saves World with Soap!*

I wasn't feeling brave at all, though. I almost wet myself as the door opened and the gruesome brain-sucking creature slimed its way toward me. I backed away from the sink, unsure of where to go . . .

Only it wasn't a two-headed alien with a hunger for boy brains at all. It wasn't even a *one*-headed alien. It was Sam Witt, furiously rubbing his eyes.

"I've been in the nature area, looking for fact cards," he explained, splashing water over his face, "and it's set off my hay fever."

"H-hay fever?" I repeated, relief flooding through my veins. "Hay fever! Oh, thank goodness for that."

Sam turned around, wet-faced, looking confused. "Are you all right? You're acting really weird." But he didn't wait for an answer. "Was that Toby I saw coming out of here a minute ago?" he asked, changing the subject. "How did he seem? Nervous? Confident?"

"I didn't really notice," I said. "I was too busy running away from the aliens in our classroom."

Sam carried on as if he hadn't heard. "Auditions are after school tonight, and we're up for the same part again. And Toby always . . . wait a minute, WHAT DID YOU SAY?"

"Aliens. In our classroom. Horrible two-headed creatures trying to take over the planet."

Sam looked frightened for all of two seconds and then burst out laughing. "Ha ha. Good one! Have you been watching old space films with your grandpa again?"

I had, of course, but that wasn't the point. "This isn't a joke, Sam. There's a two-headed alien in our classroom at this very moment."

Sam clearly wasn't convinced.

"It's true. I swear on my entire set of Goo Attack collectibles. I saw it through the door just now. He's probably tearing into your sandwich as we speak."

That got his attention all right. "My sandwich? Someone's eating my sandwich? Well, what are we waiting for? Let's go!"

Chapter 5

Ravi, 9:25 a.m.

My hands were so soapy it took me a full five minutes to open the bathroom door, and then another ten minutes to jelly-leg-shuffle back to Mr. Hargrove's room as SLOWLY as possible. I insisted we go the long way (much to Sam's frustration), heading for the playground before skirting around the outside of the building to the fire escape door. That way, we could get a sneak preview through the windows before charging in. But to be honest, I was stalling. Even with a friend by my side and Sticky Stu in my pocket, the idea of walking straight back into the aliens' lair filled me with dread. It didn't seem to bother Sam, though. He didn't care about super-slurp slime attacks or planetary takeovers. I'm not sure he even believed me. He was too focused on his sandwich.

"Come on, Ravi," he called over his shoulder as we passed a group of girls from Miss Patterson's class counting up their fact cards. They didn't seem bothered by the aliens' arrival, either. Not that there was much to see. No intergalactic fleet blocking out the sun. No silver space disks hovering above the hopscotch court. The invaders must have had their invisibility shields on high to avoid detection. "Hurry up," Sam went on. "It took me HOURS to butter all that bread. If anything's happened to my project, I'll . . . I'll . . ." It was no good. He was too worried about his beloved sandwich to even finish the sentence.

"Slow down," I told him. "We can't just rush in without a plan." That's what the clueless shopkeeper does in *Ten Light Years from Home,* and look how *that* turns out for him. One zap from the lookout alien's human fly swatter—*SPLAT!*—and he's nothing but a squished stain on the shop wall.

"But we've already got a plan," argued Sam. "Number one— get moving. And number two—SAVE MY SANDWICH!"

He didn't seem to be taking the alien threat very seriously, charging ahead like a runaway rhino. He was already almost at the window. No, it was no good. I couldn't let him face them alone. I sprinted to catch up as he pressed his face to the glass and peered in.

"Noooooooo!" he yelled, staggering back in shock. "It can't be. I don't believe it."

I placed a trembling arm round his shoulder and peered past him into the classroom.

"Holy fishing nets, Batman!" I couldn't believe it, either. The unearthly green light had disappeared, along with the two-headed alien. It was just a regular classroom again, full of regular desks and chairs.

"It's gone," said Sam, clinging to my arm for support. "I don't understand. How can it have just disappeared?"

"I don't know," I admitted. Perhaps the creature was an advance scout who had come to check out the planet. Maybe he didn't like what he found. "And I don't care, either, as long as it doesn't come back again. This calls for a celebration."

"A celebration?" Sam flung my arm away, looking like he was about to cry. "My sandwich is gone, and you want to celebrate?"

"What?" I stepped up to the window for a closer look, turning my attention to the project table at the back of the class. There was my marvelous moon landings model, there was Shaniqua's animal collage, and there was the empty space where Sam's sandwich used to be.

"I don't understand," Sam said, shaking his head in despair. "Sandwiches can't just disappear."

"Oh, yes they can," I told him, the pieces of the puzzle clicking together in my head. "And I'm guessing yours got beamed up to the mother ship for research purposes. Or maybe it disappeared straight into that alien's stomach. Yes! *That's* what the creature was doing in our classroom—looking for its lunch. Just think—your project will go down in the alien history books as their first taste of Earth food. How exciting is that?"

"Stop talking about aliens," said Sam. He didn't seem to share my enthusiasm. "This isn't one of your silly movies, Ravi. This is real life. It was a real-life sandwich, with real-life bread and real-life fillings. And now it's gone. Someone must have taken it."

No. Not someone. Some*thing*. A two-headed something with a bulging belly full of bread.

Chapter 6

Shaniqua, 7:15 a.m.

I was halfway through my bowl of Coco Paws when I heard the magic words coming from the TV in the living room: "And now it's over to roving reporter Elaine Eckbert for a special report from the zoo." News from the zoo? I almost dropped my spoon in excitement. Indy the elephant must have had her baby!

Rathbourne Zoo is my favorite place in the whole wide world, and lucky for me, I get to see it every day on my way to class. Well, I don't actually get to go in and admire the animals (that would be too lucky for words), but the south entrance is only a couple blocks from school, and sometimes the keepers will wave to me on their way into work. They know me pretty well by now because Mom and Dad got us a family pass for Christmas, and I spend every single Saturday I can there. I even used photos of some of the animals on my STEAM fair project—a giant collage of native wildlife. I had to miss my zoo trip this weekend, though, on account of my little brother Archie's birthday party, so I didn't get to see how Indy was doing.

Elephant pregnancies last for a whopping twenty-two months (imagine lugging a baby elephant around all that time!) which means she's had a *really* long wait to meet her new son or daughter. But it sounded like the baby was finally here. A brand-new baby elephant—yippee! How cool was that?

I grabbed my bowl off the table and headed into the living room, sloshing slushy chocolate paws onto the new cream carpet in my rush to catch the special report. Oops. Mom doesn't like us eating in front of the television (she's not too crazy about chocolate stains on her new floor, either, as it turns out), but she must have popped upstairs to get something. Perfect!

"Thank you," Elaine Eckbert was saying. "Yes, I'm here at the south entrance to Rathbourne Zoo. As you can see it's very calm and quiet out here at the moment, but I understand it's a different story inside. We've been getting reports of an escaped animal."

The bowl of coco paws slipped clean out of my hands, landing upside down on the new carpet with a wet *thud*. I didn't even notice at first—I was too busy looking for the remote control to turn up the volume. An escaped animal? This I *had* to hear. "Apparently a ti—"

I didn't catch the rest, unfortunately. Whatever else Elaine had to say about the escaped animal was drowned out by a high-pitched squeal of horror from the doorway. "Eeeeeeooooowww! What's that all over the floor?"

That's when I noticed the upside-down bowl of cereal at my feet, and the river of chocolate-colored milk oozing its way into the carpet. *Uh-oh.* And then I noticed Mom, standing there with her face all puffed-up and red. *Uh-oh was just the beginning.*

"Sorry, sorry, sorry," I said, scrabbling to pick up the fallen bowl. I was in trouble now—double trouble, most likely—but my mind was still whirring with what I'd just heard. An escaped ti . . . ? Oh my goodness, a tiger! It had to be.

Whoosh! Mom swooped across the room like an eastern screech owl, grabbing the remote off the armchair (so that's where it was) and switching off the TV before I could hear any more of Elaine's report.

"No, don't do that. Turn it back on," I begged. "Please. This is important. I need to hear what she says." What about the other animals—were they okay? I thought of the sweet little pygmy

goats in the petting area near the tiger enclosure, and shivered. And what about the keepers? Where was the tiger now? Still inside the zoo or out on the loose?

"And *I* need to clear up that awful brown mess on my new carpet before it stains," said Mom. "What on earth were you thinking, Shaniqua? You know you're not allowed to eat your breakfast in here."

"I know, Mom. I'm sorry, but—"

"But nothing. Go and get ready for school. You're going to be late again."

It was useless trying to argue with her when she was angry. There could have been a hundred escaped tigers prowling through the garden at that very moment, tearing up the lawn with their razor-sharp claws and peeing in the flowerbeds, and Mom still wouldn't be interested. *Not now, Shaniqua, I told you. Go and get ready for school. You're going to be late AGAIN.*

It's not like I set out to be late each morning, but time just seems to run away from me. There's always a new animal story to read in my *Weekly Wildlife* magazine or an interesting fact about meerkats or sharks or giraffes to check out in my *Ultimate Animal Encyclopedia.* And then of course there's the mini zoo under my bed: the top-secret snail and bug collection I keep hidden away behind a box of books. They all need feeding and stroking and cleaning-out (it's amazing how much poop those snails make!)

before I head off for the day. I'm not allowed any *proper* pets on account of Mom's reptile phobia (she's not exactly crazy about snails and bugs, either) and my little brother's fur allergy. One tiny sniff of animal hair and he's a-a-a-chooing into our faces like a wet, snotty firework. You should see him at the zoo if he gets too close to the lions—he becomes a one-man supersonic sneeze machine. Mind you, his allergy could come in *very* handy with an escaped tiger on the loose—like a big cat advanced warning system. I'd hear Archie achooing long before hearing the tiger's hungry roar.

Chapter 7

Shaniqua, 7:35 a.m.

As Mom predicted, I was late leaving for school again. One of my pet woodlice made a break for freedom while I was cleaning out the snail poop (he must have been inspired by the tiger at the zoo) and refused to come out from under the closet. I was in such a rush afterward that I forgot my animal collage and had to race back to the house to get it. Of course I tried telling Mom we should all stay at home today, explaining that it wasn't safe to be outside with a big cat on the loose, but she refused to listen.

"I'm not in the mood for your silly jokes this morning, Shaniqua," she said. "I *still* haven't got all the chocolate marks off the carpet and now I'm going to be late getting Archie to daycare."

"It's not a joke," I told her. "Not this time." Not like yesterday, when I told her there was an electric eel in the bath so I couldn't wash my hair. Or the day before, when I told Archie not to unwrap the big present from Grammy and Pops because there was a skunk inside, waiting to spray him with birthday stink. "There really is an escaped ti—"

"School," Mom growled, doing a pretty good impression of a tiger herself. "NOW! And don't forget to drop your consent form for track and field day in at the office when you get there."

What choice did I have? I picked up my poor, forgotten collage, tucked it under my arm, and set off for school all over again, keeping a VERY sharp eye out for any orange and black stripes heading my way.

There was no sign of roving reporter Elaine Eckbert when I passed the south gate of the zoo. The news crew must have driven her back to the studio for her own safety. And there was no sign of the missing tiger, either—phew! I'd been expecting to find the whole area marked off with police tape, together with big signs warning members of the public to keep away. But there was nothing like that. Maybe they'd caught him already, and he was tucked back in his cage where he belonged. Or maybe they were trying to keep the escape quiet to stop people from swarming the place with their cellphones, trying to snatch selfies with the dangerous animal. That's what happened when that alligator got into the car park near Grammy and Pop's house in Florida. Grammy said one lady nearly had her leg bitten off trying to snap the perfect photo. How crazy is that? And Pops told me the lady bit the alligator back, just to even things up a bit. But he's a bit of a joker, like me. I think that's where I get it from.

I wasn't in the mood for jokes this morning, though. Every rustle behind a tree or bush had me jumping like a startled kangaroo, and I nearly dropped my collage when I spotted a jogger in stripy orange leggings racing around the corner by Mr. Hargrove's house. Mr. Hargrove and my uncle play on the same ultimate Frisbee team (that's how I know where he lives), but it didn't look like my teacher would be playing ultimate any time soon, judging by the chewed-up sneaker on his front lawn. The sneaker was gecko green, with flamingo stripes down the sides, and laces (or what was left of them) in bright ladybug red. It looked exactly like the pair he'd been wearing at last Friday's practice for our upcoming track and field day . . . only they'd been all gleaming new, and this poor thing looked like it had been mauled by a pack of hungry hyenas. Or one escaped tiger.

Oh no. It couldn't be. Could it? I glanced around the garden, my heart pounding at the thought of poor Mr. Hargrove and

those terrible big cat claws and teeth. There was no sign of the other sneaker and no sign of my teacher. But I *did* spot a row of giant paw prints in one of the flower beds. That wasn't a good sign, was it?

I ran the rest of the way to school, my collage bashing into my side with every terrified step. *Please let Mr. Hargrove be all right*, I kept thinking, trying to make sense of what I'd seen. There had to be another explanation—there just had to. Even if the runaway tiger *had* gone stalking through his front garden, that didn't mean he stayed for breakfast. Of course it didn't. And then maybe Mr. Hargrove threw his sneaker to scare him off. Yes, that would make sense. The tiger must have given it a quick chew, just to check there were no tasty feet inside, and then headed back to the zoo.

I wanted to believe that's what had happened—that Mr. Hargrove would be waiting in the classroom with his usual cheery smile. I *made* myself believe it (almost, anyway). But that didn't stop my worrying. I needed to see Mr. Hargrove for myself, just to make sure he was still in one piece. I took a shortcut across the park, long-jumped over the stream, and swerved around a pair of poodles, with a final two-hundred-meter sprint to the school steps.

"Shaniqua?" asked Mrs. Penford, scuttling out of the school office like an overexcited, glorious beetle, dressed head to foot in green. Even her glasses were green today. "Whatever's the matter, dear?"

"Can't . . . stop . . . Have . . . to . . . get . . . to . . . class," I panted.

Mrs. Penford smiled. "Oh yes, it's the big treasure hunt today, isn't it? Miss Patterson was telling me all about it on the way in. No wonder you're in such a hurry!"

The treasure hunt? I'd completely forgotten about that! But I nodded anyway, anxious to get going.

"I'm glad I've caught you, though," said Mrs. Penford, slipping back into official school secretary mode. "I'm still waiting for that consent form for track and field day. You know you won't be able to take part without it."

The form! I'd forgotten about that as well. Tiger worries had pushed everything else clean out of my head. "Mom did it for me this morning," I said, grateful for the reminder. I didn't want to get in trouble for that as well. "It's in here somewhere . . ."

I was still rooting around in my bag for it, like a raccoon digging for grubs, when the phone rang. Mrs. Penford scuttled back into the office to answer it.

"Oh, hello again, Mrs. Hargrove," she said. My ears pricked up at once. "Yes, yes, I got the message, thanks. I hope everything's okay." There was a long pause followed by a sharp gasp of shock. "Good gracious! And he ate the entire leg? Poor thing, I hope he's going to be okay . . . Oh dear, that must have been a horrible sight. Listen, you tell Mr. Hargrove not to worry about his class—I've arranged for Mrs. Ample to cover for him."

So it was true, then. The tiger really *had* attacked Mr. Hargrove. And we weren't just talking about a half-chewed sneaker by the sounds of it. Not even a half-chewed toe. She said he'd eaten "the entire leg."

I couldn't bear to hear any more. Just the thought of the attack made me feel queasy. Poor, poor Mr. Hargrove. There'd be no track and field day for him this year, would there? No STEAM fair. No treasure hunt. I left my form on Mrs. Penford's desk and slunk away to break the news to everyone else.

Chapter 8

Shaniqua, 8:00 a.m.

I was on my way to class when I heard it—a terrible, blood-chilling *RRROOOOAARR.*

Oh no! The tiger!

I froze, too terrified to move, hoping against hope that I'd imagined it.

ROOOOAAARRRRRRRRRRRRRRRRRRR!

But there it was again, coming from somewhere near the

school kitchen. A long, loud roar that made the hairs on my neck stand up. There was no imagining a roar like that.

Don't panic, I told myself. *Stay calm.* (It didn't work.)

Stay calm? I argued back. *Are you crazy? There's a tiger on the loose!*

I wished I could remember what it said about tigers in my animal encyclopedia. Did a roar like that mean it was mad? Scared? Hungry? Maybe it had a taste for teachers now and had come looking for another one. Or maybe it'd just gotten a taste for legs. I had to warn my friends before it was too late.

Everyone was on their way into Miss Patterson's class when I got there, getting ready for the treasure hunt.

"Look out!" I shouted. "There's a tiger on the loose! He escaped from the zoo and he's headed this way."

But the others just laughed, acting like it was one of my jokes.

"I'm *serious*," I told them. Yes, I'd been joking about the piranha in the swimming pool. And yes, I *might* have been pulling their legs about the principal being kidnapped by clowns. But this was different. This was a matter of life and death.

It was no good, though. Not even Mrs. Ample, the substitute teacher, believed me. "I think we'd know if there was a tiger running around the school eating people, don't you?" she said, when I tried to warn her. "Now leave your project at the back with the others and hurry next door. You don't want to miss the start of the treasure hunt."

"But Mrs.—"

"But nothing," she said, growing impatient. "I don't want to hear any more of this tiger nonsense. Okay?"

But . . . but . . . "Okay," I agreed, biting back my fear and frustration. Why wouldn't anyone listen? Couldn't they tell the difference between a light-hearted joke and a full-on big-cat emergency?

I headed back to the office the moment Miss Patterson finished her list of rules. Not that I actually heard any of them. My brain was too busy making up its own set of instructions. Only it wasn't a treasure hunt I was thinking of, it was a tiger hunt:

Be quiet and keep your distance.

No going near the kitchen.

No sudden movements. (Or was that bears?)

No waving around a tin of cat food.

No stopping to tickle his tummy.

Mrs. Penford was my last hope. She knew the truth about Mr. Hargrove and his poor leg. *She'd* believe me, even if no one else did. But the school office was empty. That meant there was only one option left . . . a SUPER SCARY option: I'd have to stop the tiger myself.

Chapter 9

Shaniqua, 8:30 a.m.

I decided to head to the school library. I wanted to research tiger information to try and come up with a plan. Knowledge is power! Did you know a fully-grown tiger can weigh up to 700 pounds (that's seven times as heavy as me) and measure up to eleven feet long? Yikes! As if I hadn't been frightened enough before. And according to the library's copy of *101 Big Cat Facts,* tigers only eat meat (not sneakers, just legs) so there was no point trying to lure him into a trap with cakes from the school cafeteria. What else? They like water (so much for my giant water pistol idea) and they can reach speeds of up to thirty-six miles per hour. It didn't look like running away was much of an option, either.

As far as Totally Safe and Foolproof Ways to Save the School from a Hungry Runaway Tiger go, I wasn't making much progress. The only *good* thing I discovered was that you can hear a tiger roar from up to almost two miles away—so maybe he hadn't made it as far as the school when I heard him by the kitchens earlier. But that didn't mean he wasn't on his way now. That didn't mean he wasn't stalking his way along the hallway at that very moment, looking for another tasty leg to gnaw on.

I swapped over into the window seat after a while for a clearer view of any approaching danger (for example, an eleven-foot-long cat coming my way at thirty-six miles per hour.) It was hard reading and keeping guard at the same time, though. At one point, Ravi must have walked right past me, but I didn't notice him at first. I glanced up just as he disappeared down the hallway, head down low as if he was looking for something. Treasure hunt fact cards, I assumed.

I spotted Deena briefly too. She popped into the library sometime later, looking almost as pale and scared as I was. Maybe she'd just had a run-in with the tiger! I got my hopes up for a moment, thinking if we went to the teachers together they'd *have* to believe us, and then they could call the zoo. The keepers would know what to do. They probably had tranquilizer darts, like on that zoo vet program I watched the other week, to help turn an angry roaring tiger into an oversized sleeping kitten. But I was out of luck. Deena nearly jumped out of her skin when I called over to her, looking more terrified than ever. And then she was off, shooting back out the door without so much as a backwards glance. I was on my own for big cat catching, whether I liked it or not.

I must have been in the library a good hour or so—maybe longer—when I heard raised voices outside the door.

"For the last time, there's no such thing as sandwich-stealing aliens." It sounded like Sam.

"But I saw it with my own eyes." I recognized that voice too. It was Ravi.

"And you actually saw it take my sandwich, huh?" Sam sounded pretty annoyed. "You saw it bite into the bread with its weird alien jaws? You saw the mayonnaise and onion relish dribbling down its double chins? And the bits of lettuce stuck between its black alien teeth?"

"Well, no," said Ravi. "I didn't see the actual eating part. I was in too much of a hurry to get away." He paused. "Wait a minute, why would an alien have black teeth?"

"That's what color they are in *Dementors of the Milky Way* or whatever it was you made us watch on your birthday."

"What? They weren't dementors—you're thinking of Harry Potter." It sounded like Ravi was getting pretty annoyed too. "They were *defenders*, defending the galaxy against an army of *purple*-toothed invaders."

Sam made a funny grunting noise in his throat. "Their teeth looked pretty black from where I was sitting. Not that it matters, anyway. The point is, it wasn't a hungry alien who stole my sandwich. And it didn't get beamed up to another planet while no one was looking."

"So where is it, then?" asked Ravi. "Sandwiches don't just vanish into thin air, you know. *Someone* must have taken it. And I bet you anything it was that big, scary—"

"Tiger," I cut in, slipping out of the safe hush of the library to join them.

Sam and Ravi stared at me in surprise. "WHAT?"

"I heard you say someone's taken your sandwich. Is that right?" I knew Sam must be upset—his project *was* pretty amazing—but I was secretly pleased to hear it. That missing sandwich was proper proof of my story, evidence of a hungry tiger stalking the school hallways looking for his next snack.

Sam nodded. "Ravi thought he saw something strange in the classroom and made us go the long way around to investigate, but by then it was too late. My poor sandwich was already gone."

"I know who took it," I told him. "It was the escaped tiger

from the zoo. First he ate Mr. Hargrove's leg, and then he came here looking for his next course."

"WHAT?" they both said again, eyes bulging like a pair of tree frogs.

"The tiger," I repeated. "I tried to warn you earlier, but no one would listen. No one believed me. And *now* look what's happened."

Judging by the looks on their faces they still didn't believe me. Sam shook his head. "You're telling us there's a tiger running around, stealing sandwiches out of classrooms? That's even crazier than Ravi's alien theory."

"But I saw the paw prints in Mr. Hargrove's garden," I said. "And I heard it roaring on my way into class. And when I was in the office, I overheard Mrs. Penford on the phone with Mr. Hargrove's wife, and *she* said—"

Wait a minute. What was that? It sounded like running footsteps and a strange swishing sound. And yes, it sounded like someone whimpering with fright. *Uh-oh.*

"TIGER!" I warned the others in a loud whisper, racking my brains to remember what I'd learned from *101 Big Cat Facts.* I was trying to think of anything that might help us . . . us and the poor person heading our way with a vicious tiger on her tail. Anything at all.

The footsteps and swishing grew louder as the runner

rounded the corner into the hallway. It was Mrs. Penford! Her face was the color of a raspberry, her green glasses bouncing up and down on her nose as she puffed and panted towards us, still whimpering under her breath:

"Oh my goodness, oh my goodness, what a day!"

"You see," I hissed to Sam. "Now the tiger's moved on from sandwiches to school secretaries. What are we going to do?"

"She must be on the run from aliens," said Ravi. "They liked your sandwich so much they've come back for the rest of the planet. This is all your fault, Sam. You shouldn't have made it so tasty!"

Sam pulled a face, as if we were both completely nuts. "What's wrong, Mrs. Penford?" he asked. "What's happened?"

"It's . . . It's Mrs. Ample," she panted. "Poor lady. I must get back to her. I've just called for an ambulance. Oh my goodness. What a day. What a day." And with that, she stumbled off down the hallway, her green trouser suit swishing as she ran.

"*Now* do you believe me?" I said. "The tiger must have gotten Mrs. Ample too! If only she'd listened to me earlier."

"*Now* do you believe me?" asked Ravi. "The aliens must have turned their super-stun lasers on Mrs. Ample. No wonder she needs an ambulance. It's lucky they didn't beam her off to another planet while they were at it."

"It wasn't aliens with a stun laser," I told him, crossing my arms in front of me. "It was the tiger."

"It was aliens," Ravi insisted.

"Tiger."

"Aliens."

"Tiger."

"Aliens."

"I don't care how many times you say it. I know for a *fact* it was the tiger," I said, ending the argument once and for all. Well, it wasn't me who ended it really. It was the school librarian, on her way in from recess, who told us all to be quiet and get back to class.

"But we're not in class this morning," Sam explained. "We're doing a treasure hunt."

"Well you're not going to find any treasure standing here arguing, are you?" she said. "Off you go now. Quietly, please."

"It was aliens," Ravi whispered as we left, determined to have the last word.

"Tiger," I whispered back.

Chapter 10

Deena, 7:47 a.m.

Today was the big day. The REALLY big day. With the treasure hunt in the morning, the STEAM fair in the afternoon, and *Wizard of Oz* auditions straight after school, it was almost more excitement than I could manage. My stomach had been churning like an ice cream maker since I woke up, and by the time I got to school I felt decidedly queasy. It was probably down to nerves (I always get nervous before an audition, *especially* if I'm up for the same part as Ella Foot), with an extra helping of library-book worry to add to the mix.

I'd been so busy finishing my Famous American Actresses poster (while rehearsing my lines) that I completely forgot about the library book. It was a non-lending copy of *The Wizard of Oz*—a beautiful, big, illustrated version that I "borrowed" from the library on Friday to help me get into the role of Dorothy. It really *did* help too, although I felt bad for breaking the rules like that. Mr. Lendworthy, the school librarian, is very strict about reference only books staying in the library for everyone to read, and I wouldn't normally have dreamt of sneaking it out in my backpack while no one was looking. But I really, really want this part, and Ella Foot still hadn't returned the other copy of *The Wizard of Oz*, even though she had borrowed it weeks ago and knew I was waiting for it. If she got the part of Dorothy instead of me, I'd . . . I'd . . . Well, I didn't know what I'd do. It would probably involve screaming, though. Ella always makes me want to scream.

The plan was to sneak the stolen book back onto the shelf this morning before Mr. Lendworthy noticed it was gone. (I mean "borrowed," not "stolen"—that makes it sound even worse.) Yes, that was the plan. It was a pretty foolproof plan too—at least it would have been if the book wasn't still tucked under my pillow at home. Yellow Brick Road Blocks! That wasn't good. That wasn't good at all.

It was too late by the time I realized. Mom had already dropped me off at the steps and driven off, so I headed into school without it, hoping for the best. What choice did I have? Maybe Mr. Lendworthy would be too busy ordering new books to check the shelves today. That's what I told myself. Maybe he wouldn't spot the big *Wizard of Oz*-shaped gap between *The Bumper Book of Classic American Tales* and *How to Train Your Flying Monkey* (or whatever it was called). Maybe, just maybe, I'd get away with it. The one thing I knew for certain was that I had to get a grip on myself and stop worrying, otherwise I'd risk messing up my audition. And then Ella would get to be Dorothy in the school play and I'd never EVER hear the end of it.

Luckily there was plenty to take my mind off the missing book: paintings, poems, craft-stick bridges, and even a stuffed alligator head! (It was a good thing Shaniqua arrived too late to see *that*. I don't think she'd have approved.) Ravi had done a space-themed project (no surprise there). Mateo had written an entire recipe book (no surprise there either). And Sam . . . well, Sam had made the most amazing-looking sandwich in the world. It was incredible! That sandwich deserved a place in the *Guinness Book of Records*. It deserved a whole page just to itself. Thinking about the *Guinness Book of Records* got me thinking about library reference books again. Not for long, though, because the substitute teacher sent us all next door to Miss Patterson's class to get ready for the treasure hunt, and there was Ella Foot, looking as smug and full of herself as always.

"Hello, Dinner," she said, smiling that smarmy I'm-better-than-you smile of hers. She knows perfectly well that's not how you say my name—she only does it to bug me. It works too. Being called "Dinner" annoys me more than anything, but I try not to let *her* see that. I pretend I can't care less what she calls me, even while I'm seething inside. It's all good practice for my acting.

"Hello, Ella," I replied, giving her my very best you-don't-scare-me smile in return. "All ready for your audition this afternoon?"

"Ready to snatch the part of Dorothy out from under your nose, you mean?" She gave a little laugh. "You bet. Don't worry, Dinner, I'm sure there's a spare munchkin part for you. Or maybe you could play the Tin Man? That might suit your short hair and stiff acting a bit better."

And you'd be better off playing the Wicked Witch of the West, I thought, but didn't say it out loud. I decided not to stoop to her level, even if I *was* fantasizing about tipping a bucket of water over her head, like Dorothy does to the witch at the end of the play. *Take that, Evil Ella of the East.*

"May the best man win," I said instead, slipping into the

voice of an English gentleman and dropping into a low bow. *I'll show you*, I was thinking, a fresh buzz of determination fizzing through my veins. Just because I didn't have Ella's long, silky hair and perfectly ribboned pigtails didn't mean I couldn't say the lines as well as her. And the fact that I preferred wearing boys' clothes to girly dresses didn't mean I couldn't sing the songs just as beautifully. I'd been practicing "Somewhere Over the Rainbow" for so many weeks I could sing it forward, backward, and standing on my head. I even knew the Spanish version! I had as much chance of scooping that starring role as anyone, *especially* Ella Foot.

"The best *girl,* don't you mean?" she said. "And we all know who that is." She twisted the end of one of her pigtails and smoothed down her blue pinafore dress, as if to prove what a natural Dorothy she was. Huh! Well, I had a couple of Dorothy connections of my own: Mom's family can trace their roots back to the Pawnee tribe, meaning I've got proper Kansas blood in my family. *And* I'd borrowed my big sister's glittery, red sneakers for the day, which were much more like Dorothy's ruby slippers than the silly, frilly sandals Ella was wearing. Not that she'd even noticed—she was too busy showing off as usual.

"The part's as good as mine," she said, sticking her chin in the air. "*Especially* after what I discovered."

"Quiet, girls," called Miss Patterson, fixing us with such a steely stare that we sat in silence for the rest of her how-to-look-for-fact-cards talk. Who knew there was so much to say on the subject? "And the class that collects the most cards wins," she eventually finished. "Now enjoy the treasure hunt, everyone, but make sure you stick to the rules:

Be quiet and respectful of other classes.

No practicing songs in the hallways.

No scarecrow dancing.

No flying monkey impressions.

Follow the yellow brick road.

The rules went *something* like that, anyway. If I'm honest, I'd sort of stopped listening by the end. I was too busy wondering what Ella had discovered. A secret spell for wowing the teachers on the casting panel? A squished wicked witch under the basement of her house? Magic nose hairs sprouting out of her nostrils?

"And no surrender!" said Ravi, under his breath, when Miss Patterson finally, *finally* stopped talking. He made the treasure hunt sound like a battle for survival.

"No waving around a tin of cat food," murmured Shaniqua, as if that should have been on the list of rules as well (although I'm not sure what good cat food would be in a treasure hunt). "No stopping to tickle his tummy."

"No thinking about that sandwich," added Mateo. "That delicious, succulent sandwich. *Mmmm, sandwich . . .*"

It seemed like everyone had their own version of the rules to see them through the hunt that morning, including me:

Don't forget to wish Sam good luck for his audition.

Don't get your sister's sneakers dirty.

Don't think about the missing library book.

Whatever you do, don't think about the missing library book.

Chapter 11

Deena, 8:20 a.m.

The first fact card was easy to spot: *The famous Oscar statuette is 13.5 inches tall and weighs 8.5 pounds.* It was right there on the bulletin board outside the performance hall, above the sign-up list for *Wizard of Oz* auditions, as if some of us might be Oscar winners too, one day. How amazing would that be? Maybe I'd give Ella a special mention in my acceptance speech.

And lastly, I'd like to thank Ella Foot, for her endless put-downs when we were at school together. I still remember the time she told

*me I'd never get the main part in our school play because I was
too much of a tomboy and that I looked more like the Tin Man
with my short hair than Dorothy. But her nasty comments made
me more determined than ever. I decided to prove that acting's not
about looks and outfits—it's about talent and hard work. It's that
same determination that's got me where I am today. I might not be
standing up here with this lovely Oscar if it wasn't for the likes of
Ms. Foot. Thank you, Ella!*

I could already hear the applause ringing in my ears . . . and
then my gaze dropped down to the sheet below and the clapping
faded away to nothing. I'd been the first person to sign up for
Dorothy (the first person to sign up for any of the parts, for that
matter), but Ella had squeezed her name into the gap ahead of
mine, the last few letters of "Foot" covering over the start of
"Deena" in bright-pink pen. I felt a familiar burst of annoyance as
I stood there staring at it, my Oscar-winning daydream popping
like an over-inflated balloon. What did it matter where anyone's
name came on the list? It was only a stupid sign-up sheet. Why
did Ella always have to make everything into a competition?
*My long legs make me so much faster at front crawl . . . my lunch
looks* so *much tastier than yours . . . my mean streak makes me ten
times as horrible as you . . .* Mind you, the other students in Miss
Patterson's class were almost as bad, gloating like mad when they

beat us at sports or spelling bees, or simply just nabbing the best seats in the cafeteria.

I skimmed down the list, spotting lots of familiar names from past productions. Sam was down for the role of Scarecrow. I knew he'd be brilliant at the part (he was even better at acting than he was at sandwich-making), and rehearsals would be doubly fun if I got to play Dorothy next to him. He'd have to beat Toby Fishwick first, though. Toby was another of the we're-better-than-you kids in Miss Patterson's class, and he and Sam *always* seemed to go for the same role, no matter what the play was. Last year, it was a musical production of *The Toys that Talked,* and Toby still hadn't forgiven Sam for scooping the part of the singing robot dog, leaving him to play the evil inventor.

I tucked the Oscar fact card into my pocket and slipped into the back of the hall, planning on a sneaky run-through of my audition piece while no one was around. That way, it wouldn't seem quite so scary when I performed it for real after school. That was the theory, anyway. But I was out of luck. *Seriously* out of luck. Someone had gotten to the stage ahead of me . . . someone in a blue pinafore dress and pigtails, singing "Somewhere Over the Rainbow" and looking very pleased with herself. *Meddling Munchkins!* How had Ella snuck past me?

I slunk back out of sight, my heart sinking further and further as I watched her from the shadows. It must have been halfway to

my feet by the time she reached the perfect final note, basking in an unseen spotlight as her imaginary orchestra died away to nothing. Wow! That was good. Really good. She stood there for a while afterward, clutching her cuddly Toto dog to her chest, lashes fluttering above her big brown eyes. She didn't just *look* like Dorothy—she *was* Dorothy. How could I compete with that? Maybe her monologue, the second part of her audition, would be less impressive.

"And now I'd like to perform a short extract from *Lock 'Em Up and Throw Away the Key*," Ella said, putting down the stuffed dog and moving to the front of the stage. She cleared her throat, smiled to the imaginary panel of teachers, and began.

"I didn't steal it," she whimpered in a scared-sounding voice. "You have to believe me. I only ever meant to borrow it . . ."

What? I thought about the library book nestled under my pillow at home and swallowed hard. It could almost have been a play about *me*.

"I've been feeling guilty about it ever since. I know it's just a book, but . . ."

This was starting to get spooky. It was like she could read my mind.

"Please don't send me to jail," Ella finished, clasping her hands together as if she was begging for mercy. "I promise I'll never do it again . . ."

"How did you know?" The words were out of my mouth before I could stop them. I stepped out of the shadows and headed for the stage.

"How did I know about the stolen reference book?" asked Ella, looking more pleased with herself than ever. "I was there in the library. I saw you take it, just like I saw you coming in here now when you're supposed to be doing the treasure hunt. You're not very good at sneaking around, are you?"

Cold sweat trickled down my back. "You won't tell anyone, will you? About the library book, I mean. I was going to bring it back today, but I forgot."

Ella rested her hands on her hips. "Well, Dinner, that depends, doesn't it? How about we make a deal? I won't say anything about the STOLEN library book if you agree to audition for another part instead?"

"That's not fair. I . . . I . . ." I couldn't give up my Dorothy dream now. I just couldn't. The very thought sent tears running down my cheeks, dripping onto my glittery, red sneakers. But what choice did I have? If Mr. Lendworthy found out I'd taken one of his precious library books, he'd . . . Actually, I didn't know *what* he'd do. Tell my parents? Tell the principal? Tell the police? I could already see the headlines in the local newspaper: *DESPERATE DEENA IN BOOK-STEALING STORM*. I could already see the disappointment in Dad's face as he read the article over his morning eggs . . . the disappointment in *everyone's* faces.

"I'll give you some time to think about it," said Ella, smiling sweetly as if she was doing me a favor. "Come and find me after our class wins the treasure hunt and let me know what you've decided."

I opened and closed my mouth like a surprised goldfish, trying to bend my lips around the right words. *I'm not scared of you, Ella Foot. You can't bully me out of my rightful role.* But nothing came out. I *was* scared, that was the problem. I was scared and angry and confused and a hundred other feelings all buzzing around inside my head at the same time. If *only* I'd remembered that library book. No, if only I'd left it on the reference shelf in the first place.

"See you later, Dinner," chirped Ella, skipping toward the door. "Enjoy the treasure hunt."

Huh! It wasn't hidden fact cards I needed to find, it was courage. And brains to help me figure out the best thing to do. And maybe a new heart while I was at it, since mine was beating fast enough to burst.

"Nice shoes, by the way," she called back over her shoulder as she left. "Maybe I can borrow them for the play? It's not like you'll be needing them."

Chapter 12

Deena, 8:55 a.m.

I sat on the edge of the stage afterward, sniffling into a tissue and trying to decide what to do. It didn't get me very far, though. At first, I was ready to admit defeat and audition for a smaller part instead—who wouldn't want to be a munchkin, anyway?—but then I decided to call Ella's bluff and see what she'd do. After all, it's not like I actually *stole* the library book. I was only borrowing it. Mr. Lendworthy would understand, wouldn't he? But what if he didn't? Perhaps it was too risky.

By ten to nine, I had run out of tissues (and patience). Sitting there, going around in circles—yes, no, yes, no—wasn't getting me anywhere.

"Come on, Deena Locklear," I said in my best squeaky squirrel voice (that always cheers my little sister up when she's upset, especially if it comes with a tickle.) "Don't listen to Ella. She's one baaaaaaaad nut. You'll find a way out of this mess. You always do." But it was no good. There was another little voice inside my head—a voice that sounded suspiciously like Ella—that refused to listen. "You might as well give up now, Dinner," it said. "No more Dorothy for you."

I thought about all the famous Hollywood actresses on my STEAM fair poster. *They* didn't give up on their dreams, did they? But then again, I bet they never got expelled for stealing a library book, either. Of all the people who might have spotted me slipping it into my bag on Friday, why did it have to be Ella?

Maybe all I needed was a bit of fresh air. Yes, a nice bit of fresh air to clear my head and help me think straight. That was the plan, anyway.

I used the exit behind the stage and headed to the playing fields. As I was passing the boy's bathroom, I heard a horrible sound coming through the open window. No, not *that* kind of horrible bathroom sound. This was a high-pitched screeching noise, like someone trying to strum an electric guitar with a live cat.

"I don't know why I didn't think of it before!" said a voice, after the guitar-screeching had finished. Whoever it was, he sounded pretty excited about something. "It's the perfect plan. He'll be so upset when he realizes it's gone, that he won't be able to perform, and victory will be mine, all mine." Then came a laugh, and not just a passing giggle, either. This was a full-on evil cackle.

That's when I realized who the voice belonged to: Toby Fishwick. It had to be. I *thought* it sounded familiar, and I recognized that laugh from last year's play. It was the same dastardly chuckle that Toby's evil inventor character let out as he tied the toy robot dog to the wooden railway tracks. But what was Toby *doing* in there? Planning a daring toilet paper robbery? Plotting to steal the soap? *He'll be so upset when he realizes he can't wash his hands properly, that he'll crumple into a germy heap and victory will be mine, all mine . . .* And what was that strangled-cat-guitar noise supposed to be? Where did that fit into his peculiar plan?

I didn't get the chance to find out because I could see Mrs. Ample waddling towards me with a funny screwed-up look on her face—like she was really angry (or really constipated). *Eek!* I was in enough trouble already without adding "listening outside the boys' bathroom" to the list, so I turned and ran . . . all the way past the playground to the end of the playing fields where

no one could find me. Down to the Hiding Tree with its empty hollow, the perfect place to escape angry teachers and spiteful rivals. And maybe if I hid away in there long enough, everyone would forget about the missing library book too.

There was just one problem—the empty hollow wasn't empty after all. There was a treasure hunt fact card waiting for me inside:

Did you know, read the card, *that the hallways in Alcatraz prison were named after major American streets such as Broadway (a New York Street famous for its theaters) and Michigan Avenue?*

No, I hadn't known that. But reading it sent a funny shiver down my spine as if the card was trying to tell me something: *The only Broadway you'll be starring on at this rate is a prison hallway.*

That's when I realized I needed to come clean, to admit what I'd done and apologize, before things got any more out of hand. I might have made a mistake (a big, book-shaped mistake), but I wasn't a criminal. So why was I acting like one? Hiding away like a robber on the run—like a cowardly lion—wasn't going to solve anything, was it? Besides, Mr. Lendworthy deserved to know the truth, rather than Ella's twisted version of events.

I took a deep breath and started back up the field toward the school, full of bravery and good intentions.

You can do this, I told myself. *Think how much better you'll feel when it's all out in the open. Think about the look on Ella's face when she realizes you've already come clean.* But my resolve grew weaker with every step. What if Mr. Lendworthy refused to listen to my side of the story? What if they packed me off to Book Stealer's Detention before I got the chance to explain? What if . . .?

I found myself thinking of the time that fourth-grader got caught stealing from the Save the Animals charity box and wasn't allowed to go to activities camp anymore. What if they did the same to me, or something even worse? What if they banned me from being in the school play altogether, to teach me a lesson? *No. Please. Anything but that!*

Not being allowed to act was almost too awful to imagine. But that's exactly what I was doing as I headed inside—imagining myself stuck in the back row of the audience watching Ella Foot prance her way along the yellow brick road. I imagined myself mouthing Dorothy's lines under my breath, wishing I'd never set eyes on that book. And I imagined Mom turning to me during intermission, whispering, "That could have been you up there, Deena. If only you hadn't been a thief."

By the time I reached the library, I'd imagined myself into a nervous wreck. But I summoned up what tiny scraps of courage I had left and pushed open the door.

Chapter 13

Deena, 9:15 a.m.

This was it, then. Back to the scene of the crime. *Hello, library. It's me, again, Deena Locklear, rule-breaker, book-stealer, and champion worrier. I've come to make things right. That's if it's not too late already* . . . If the red sneakers on my feet were magic, like Dorothy's ruby slippers, I'd have clicked my heels together three times and wished myself away again, just like that. But the only special power my sister's shoes had ever possessed was the power to stink up the house after she stepped in something nasty in the park. And even *that* power stopped working once Mom scrubbed them clean and sprayed them with disinfectant. Not that a magical super-stench would have been much use to me just then, anyway. It would take more than a bad smell to get me out of this one.

The library was deathly quiet, as quiet as a theater when the curtain goes up, or as a film with the sound turned off. As quiet as . . . well, as a library, I guess. On the plus side, that probably meant the place was empty. The last thing I wanted was a crowd of onlookers listening in on my confession. But on the downside, it meant I could hear my own heart pounding inside my chest, reminding me how nervous I was:

B-boom, b-boom, b-boom,

BA-BOOM, BA-BOOM, **BA-BOOM!**

It was so quiet I could hear my shoes rubbing on the carpet as I forced myself on, one trembling step at a time . . . *sh-swish, sh-swish, sh-swish* . . . I could hear the irritating buzz of a fly from somewhere near the comfy cushion corner. *Gulp.* That's where I'd been sitting with the *Wizard of Oz* book when I first decided to "borrow" it for the weekend. And there, right next to it, was the reference shelf itself, with a hole where the missing book should be. There was the carousel of nonfiction books I almost sent flying in my rush to get away afterward. And there was Mr. Lendworthy's desk, where fate was waiting for me. His empty desk.

What? Where was he? How could I explain what I'd done if there was no one there to explain to? Maybe Ella had changed her mind about giving me time to think. Maybe she'd spilled the beans already, and the librarian was out scouring the school for me at that very moment. In which case it was too late. I was doomed. DOOMED!

You know what they say about your life flashing before your eyes when you think you're going to die? This was a bit like that, only without the dying part at the end. And it wasn't my whole life flashing before my eyes, just the events of that morning. It was like speeding through TV commercials on super fast-forward, with me as the star of each one: there I was rushing out of the house without the library book . . . there we all were, crowded around Sam's incredible sandwich . . . there was Ella laughing at me from the stage . . . there was the hollow in the old tree, with the watch-out-you-don't-end-up-in-prison fact card . . . and there I was now, frozen with fear in the middle of the library, like a deer caught in car headlights, or a deer listening to hunters getting closer and closer and—

"Deena!"

I swear I leapt five feet in the air when I heard my name. I turned and ran, racing out of the library, down the hallway, around the corner, past the school office, and out into the sunshine . . . to see a police patrol car waiting out front.

It was all over. That's what I thought at first, anyway, sinking down to the warm sidewalk in despair. They'd clearly come to take me away, just like in that cop show Dad lets me watch with him when Mom's at her book club. I'd watched enough episodes of *Manhattan 369* to know *exactly* how the story went once the cops showed up. There was no point running now—the bad guys on Dad's show never escaped, no matter how many crowded streets or alleyways they raced down. It didn't matter how many wire fences and brick walls they leapt over, the chase always ended with an arrest. It ended with their hands cuffed behind their back and the police guiding them into the back seat of the patrol car. And after that . . . Actually, I didn't really know what came after that, apart from the credits and the hard rock theme song, but it looked like I was about to find out.

I buried my face in my hands, eyes shut tight against the full horror of it all, and waited for them to come and get me. *Goodbye, school,* I thought miserably. *Goodbye, treasure hunts and enormous sandwiches. Goodbye, end-of-term plays and proud parents clapping in the audience.* There'd be nothing like that in Book Stealers' Prison.

I sat and waited for the dreaded words: *Deena Locklear? You're being arrested on suspicion of stealing a library book from the reference shelf.* But somehow the words never came. I waited and waited and waited and still nothing happened, so I opened my eyes and looked around. The police car was empty now and so was the playground, apart from a couple of treasure hunters from Miss Patterson's class. The cops must have walked right past me, which could only mean one thing. They weren't there for me at all!

It wasn't until I got back to class later that I realized who they had *really* come for. It was Toby. Toby Fishwick. Once I heard the shocking news about Sam's stolen sandwich, all the pieces of the puzzle fell into place. *That's* what Toby had been plotting in the boy's bathroom—it all made sense now: *"It's the perfect plan. He'll be so upset when he realizes it's gone, that he won't be able to perform, and victory will be mine, all mine."* (Evil cackle, evil cackle.)

Everyone in our class had been talking about that sandwich after Mrs. Ample took attendance. Toby must have been listening in, noting how much it meant to Sam. And that's when he came up with his fiendish plan—to steal the sandwich and throw off Sam's audition. Sam would be too lost in his own buttered grief to give a convincing performance, leaving Toby free to swoop in and steal the Scarecrow part for himself. Wow. As fiendish plans went, I had to admit this was a good one, even better than Evil Ella's blackmail plot. Except something must have gone wrong. Someone must have caught Toby in the act and called the police.

My relief at not getting carted off to jail (at least not yet) was short-lived, once I heard what had happened. Poor Sam. He *loved* that sandwich. We all did. And where was it now? Swimming around in Toby's tummy? Flushed down the toilet in the boy's bathroom? Hidden in a handy gap on the library reference shelf? I might have solved *one* mystery by working out who the thief was, but that was only half the story, wasn't it? Where, oh where, was that sandwich?

Chapter 14

Mateo, 7:00 a.m.

Yuck, that looks disgusting.

That was my first thought when I sat down to breakfast this morning. It's my first thought when I sit down to breakfast *every* morning, nowadays. Mom's been on this horrible family health drive since Easter, cutting out all high-fat, sugary foods and replacing them with "nutritious alternatives." I know it's a good idea in theory—that a better diet makes people feel better all around—but Mom's taken it a bit far, if you ask me.

She spends hours every day toiling over recipes from her new *Sugar-Free, Fat-Free, Taste-Free* cookbook (at least, that's what I call it), and the results all come out the same: yuck. Sorry, that's a bit unfair. There's actually *two* flavors of yuck to choose from: tasteless cardboard yuck or cabbage mush yuck. I'm not sure which one's worse.

This morning's breakfast somehow managed to be both at the same time: dry cardboard pellets in a slimy green slop. It looked more like shriveled-up slugs floating in a sludge of liquidized caterpillars than anything resembling food. Like dehydrated cockroaches in rotten vegetable gunk. The sight of it was bad enough, especially first thing in the morning, but the smell . . . Oh my goodness, the smell. *Yuck, yuck, and double yuck.*

Dad shot me a sympathetic look as I sat down at the table, as if to say, *Sorry, Son, there was nothing I could do to stop her.* But he slipped back into a fake smile when Mom joined us, saying, "Mmm, this looks lovely, sweetheart. What is it, exactly?"

Mom beamed. "It's a new one today—date and bran energy clusters with spirulina and chia seed smoothie, plus a bonus bit of leftover cabbage juice for an extra kick."

"Spiru-what?" asked Dad.

"Spirulina," she repeated. "It's a kind of algae. It's *very* good for you. Trust me, you'll feel like a million dollars after a bowl of this."

Dad's fake smile slipped a little at the edges. I guessed he was thinking the same as me: *Algae? Isn't that the stuff we scoop off the fish pond in the garden?* And I was pretty sure neither of us would be feeling like a million dollars after a bowl of Pond Surprise. Not even a million cents. Not even one cent, come to that. The only thing *I'd* be feeling was sick.

"Oh, right. I see. That sounds, er . . . interesting," said Dad, prodding the foul-looking mixture with his spoon. I bet he missed his morning toast and jelly as much as I missed my Choco-Caramel Breakfast Boulders.

Mom was still beaming away, like she'd just won Best Chef of the Year. "I've left a bookmark in the page for you, Mateo, in case you wanted the recipe for your project. You might have to guess when it comes to how much cabbage juice you include, though. I forgot to measure it out before I stirred it in."

What? Not likely! I'd spent weeks working on my *Favorite American Recipes* book for the STEAM fair. All my favorites were in there—all the dishes I'm going to cook when I have my own diner. There was meatloaf, mac 'n' cheese, fried chicken, potato salad, creamed corn, chocolate brownies, apple pie, pancakes . . . Mmm, pancakes with crispy bacon and maple syrup . . . I'd have given anything for a plate of those instead of the Dried Slug and Fish-Poo Poison waiting for me in my bowl. No way would I be spoiling my lovely book with such a disgusting recipe.

"I don't think there's room for more recipes," I said, not wanting to hurt Mom's feelings. "Besides, I'm not sure it would go with the others. It doesn't sound very American to me."

Mom didn't take the hint. "I could even give you a little tub of it to take in as a demonstration," she said. "I'm sure Mr. Hargrove would *love* to try some."

Hmm. I was pretty sure he wouldn't. I was ninety-nine percent sure he'd rather eat his own sneakers than risk anything out of Mom's *Fun-Free Family Recipe Book of Doom*. I know I would. But lucky for Mr. Hargrove, Mom was distracted just then by the arrival of my big sister, Catalina, on her way to the hospital for an ultrasound of her baby. Her husband Patrick was away on business so Mom had offered to accompany her to the appointment instead. And she was *seriously* excited about the whole thing. You could tell by the long rush of words that came pouring out of her without even stopping for breath.

"Cat!" Mom cried, leaping up from the table to help her into a chair. "You're early! Oh my goodness. Is everything okay? How are you feeling? You look good, really good. And how's my little granddaughter doing today?"

"We won't know if it's a girl until after the scan," said Catalina, smiling at Mom's enthusiasm.

"Oh, it's a girl all right," said Mom. "I can feel it in my bones. You'll have to start thinking of names. What about Katrina? Or Christina? Georgina? Emelina?" She seemed particularly drawn to names ending in -ina. I bet if I'd been a girl, she'd have called me Matina. Or something even worse, like Marlina or Ballerina. *Concertina . . . Hyena . . . Trampolina . . .*

"Semolina?" suggested Dad, winking at me across the table. "Spirulina?"

Mom glared at him. "Don't be so silly. You can't call a baby Spirulina." Unfortunately, that seemed to remind her about breakfast. "Come on, Mateo, eat up," she said. "You can't be late for school. What about you, Cat? Can I interest you in a delicious healthy bowl of date and bran energy clusters with spirulina and chia seed smoothie?"

"I had breakfast before I came, thanks," said Cat, eyeing my bowl with suspicion. "Though I wouldn't say no to a couple cookies."

Mom leapt into action, pulling out a secret packet of cookies from the back of the cupboard. *What? How come Cat got to have cookies?*

"And some hot chocolate to dip them in, if you have any," said Cat. "I've been craving chocolate all morning."

Dad's eyes were as round as mine when he saw those cookies. To think we'd been chewing our way through Mom's cardboard-flavored Nut, Seed, and Wood-Shaving Bars for the last few weeks while there were proper cookies in the house, with real-life chocolate chips!

"Of course, darling," said Mom, producing a tub of hot chocolate from the same secret hiding spot. "If that's what you're craving, then that's what you'll have. Take the whole packet if you want. After all, you're eating for two now!"

I couldn't believe it. "How come Cat gets to have real food and we have to eat this?" I asked, giving the green gloop a nervous stir. "Ow!" I added as Dad kicked me under the table. "I mean, not that this *isn't* delicious, it's just . . ."

"You can't argue with cravings," said Mom, as if "cravings"

was a person rather than a feeling. *Hello, my name's Mr. Craving. I'm here for the cookies. ALL the cookies. Now do as I say and no arguing.* "It was pickles for me," she went on, with a dreamy look in her eye. "I went through a jar of them a day when I was pregnant with you."

"It's true," said Dad. "She was burping vinegar fumes for weeks."

Mom took no notice. "Anyway," she said, snapping out of her pickle daydream. "Cat's a big girl now. She can look after her own diet. Whereas you"—she pointed at me and Dad as if we were both kids—"still need a steer in the right direction. I know sugar withdrawal can be a bit of a shock to the system, but you'll thank me for it later."

I would? When would that be? How much later were we talking here? This afternoon? Next week? Fifty years? "Thank you wasn't really the first thing that sprang to mind when I sat down at the kitchen table these days. And it wasn't the second thing, either. Or the third. In fact, I couldn't remember eating anything meriting a true, heartfelt thank you for a long time.

"Pssst," said Cat, passing me a cookie under the table.

"Thank you," I whispered back. *Thank you, thank you, thank you.*

Chapter 15

Mateo, 7:40 a.m.

I spent the car ride to school leafing through the pages of my recipe book and dreaming about the delicious food inside. I'd managed to include a different dish or ingredient for every state, from Kentucky fried chicken and Massachusetts clam chowder to hazelnuts from Oregon and key lime pie from Florida. Mmm, key lime pie. Just a quick glance at the first ingredient—graham crackers—was enough to make my mouth water. It was enough to make my tummy rumble too, although that might have been due to skipping breakfast. As far as Mom was concerned, I'd polished off the lot in record time (fingers crossed that didn't encourage her to make it again), but two spoons of the stuff had been more than enough for me. I fed the rest to Popsy under the table while Mom was busy thinking up even more names ending in "-ina." *Nina, Mina, Tambourina.* Lucky for me, it turns out dogs LOVE chewy cardboard slug lumps in green fish goo. (Lucky for Dad too, as he was next in line with his bowl.)

By the time I got to class, I was in full fantasy mode, daydreaming about opening my diner, about the crowds clamoring to get in and taste my dishes, and about the tantalizing smells drifting out of the kitchen. I'd use the finest, most delicious ingredients—not a single leaf of cabbage on the whole menu—with amazing combinations to tickle people's taste buds. Oh yes, they'd be lining up around the block for a table once word got out about my fabulous dishes. *You must try Mateo's popping-candy apple-pie ice cream*, customers would say. *It's the tastiest dessert in town. It's the tastiest dessert on the planet!* And then I'd probably get my own cooking show on television, with a series of spin-off recipe books, and then . . . and then nothing. That's when the daydream popped like overblown bubblegum. Because that was the moment I first saw Sam's project.

Bony macaroni! That was one awesome sandwich. It had EVERYTHING: golden crusted bread, a firm, sturdy structure and fabulous fillings. It was a marvel on a plate, the sandwich to end all sandwiches. Seriously, if life were a movie, there'd have been trumpets and drums playing as Sam paraded the sandwich into class, with fireworks exploding above its big, bready head. And then a deep, booming voiceover saying, "Behold the Eighth Wonder of the World," as we all bowed down before the mouth-watering marvel that was Sam Witt's super sandwich.

I couldn't stop looking at it. I never knew Sam was such a good chef. He must have been up all night, slicing and buttering and balancing all those different fillings . . . Maybe he could come and work in my diner! I wished *I'd* thought of cooking a recipe instead of just collecting them. Boy, did I wish I'd thought of that. I could have made a huge, five-layer cake—no, wait, ten layers—dripping with sweet, creamy frosting and groaning under the weight of all the sugary decorations on top. Mom doesn't let me do much baking anymore, not unless it's one of her horrible cabbage cake recipes, but it would be different if it were for a school project. She couldn't argue with *that*.

I was still marveling over Sam's sandwich when we all went next door to Miss Patterson's room. I was already counting down the hours until the fair in the hope I might get to sample some of Sam's beautiful creation. (That's if Mrs. Ample didn't eat it first. I saw the way she was looking at it as we left the classroom.) I didn't need to be a professional chef to know it would taste a million times better than the so-called sandwiches Mom had packed for my lunch. My sandwiches didn't even have any bread. They were made of rice cakes (for the dry, dusty, cardboard taste) squished together with thick dollops of cabbage and chia seed spread (for the mush), plus sugar-free rock buns and an apple for dessert. The apple was fine, obviously. I like apples. (In fact, I was so hungry I'd slipped the apple into my trouser pocket to eat during the treasure hunt.) But Mom's rock buns were more like baseballs than food . . . to be thrown rather than eaten. One bite and all your teeth would fall out. And as for the cabbage spread? It smelled like wet mop mixed with slug graveyard, or at least what I imagined a slug graveyard would smell like. But then I remembered what Mrs. Ample had said about prizes for the winning class and I started on a brand-new daydream instead.

I imagined staggering back into class like a hero, my pockets dragging on the ground with the weight of all my treasure hunt fact cards. I imagined the triumphant cheer of my classmates as I emptied them out onto Miss Patterson's desk, claiming our rightful victory and prize. And what a prize it was. I imagined a giant treasure chest of food: of cardboard-free sandwiches with non-mush fillings, of pizzas and lasagnas and cabbage-less salads with real-life dressing, of chips and muffins and chocolate bars. I was so busy daydreaming I didn't catch what Miss Patterson was saying, but I got the gist of the rules, I think:

Be respectful of the different flavors.

No runny sauce on your clothes. (Or was it no crumbs in the hallway?)

No rushing. (Good point—it's important to chew properly.)

No snacking in the bathroom.

No thinking about that sandwich!

Chapter 16

Mateo, 9:50 a.m.

You know that saying, "Time flies when you're having fun?" It's true. I was concentrating so hard on the treasure hunt that I didn't notice the morning slipping past. I couldn't believe it was almost ten o'clock when I paused to eat my apple.

The search had been going great up until that point. I'd found seven fact cards already! If the rest of the class were doing as well as I was, we had an excellent chance of winning. I hadn't seen many of my classmates during the hunt, though, at least not to talk to—I'm not sure they even noticed me. Ravi was on the jungle gym when I spotted him (so I knew not to check there), and Shaniqua seemed to have the library covered. Who else did I see? Oh, yes, Deena, that's right. She was coming out of the performance hall looking very upset. I thought *I* was taking the hunt seriously, but she was in tears when she hurried past, which I guessed meant there were no cards to find in there. And even though I didn't *see* Sam, I thought I heard him shouting in the distance. Something about sandwich thieves and aliens, it sounded like. Very strange. But not as strange as what happened next.

I was just putting my apple core in the bin, ready for round two of fact card hunting, when I heard a strange groaning noise coming from the outdoor eating area. It sounded like a ghost in a cartoon, or a cat with its tail caught in a door. Or maybe both of them mixed together: a groaning ghost cat?

"Ooooooooowwwww. OOOOOOOOWWWWWWWW!" Whoever, or whatever, it was making such a racket, they didn't sound very happy. I hurried over to see if they needed help, my mind whirring. Maybe it was a cat with indigestion? My stomach howls a bit like that after one of Mom's cabbage stews.

It wasn't a cat, though. It was Mrs. Ample, looking like she'd eaten an entire saucepan of Mom's infamous stew. As if she'd eaten an entire wheelbarrow of the stuff. She was doubled up over one of the picnic benches, moaning

and groaning to herself. "Ooooooooowwwwwwwwwwwww. Ooooooooowwwwwwwwwwwwwwwwww."

"Are you okay?" It was a stupid question, obviously. She looked about as okay as Nana Maria when she had that explosive vomiting bug last Christmas, but I didn't know what else to say.

Mrs. Ample didn't seem to know what to say, either. She just groaned again by way of an answer, her screwed-up face all wet and shiny with sweat. For a moment I thought she might have caught the explosive vomiting bug too, but there was no evidence of any "explosions" on the grass. It couldn't be that, then, if the state of Nana Maria's splattered carpet had been anything to go by.

"Did you fall? Have you hurt yourself?" I asked, checking for signs of blood or swollen limbs.

Mrs. Ample shook her head.

"Is it stomach cramps? I get those sometimes, especially after Mom's cabbage and raisin pie."

"Ooooooooooooooowwwwwwwwwwwww."

"Or trapped gas? Her Cabbage and Bean Delight is a killer for that. Have you tried squeezing out a—" I stopped myself just in time, letting the unspoken word hang in the air between us like a bad smell. I couldn't ask a teacher *that*.

"Wait a minute," I said, remembering the funny look on Mrs. Ample's face when we left the classroom . . . the funny look she was giving Sam's sandwich. Perhaps she'd had a pregnancy craving, like Cat. I mean, who *wouldn't* get cravings for a sandwich like that? I'd been craving it all morning, and I wasn't even pregnant! She must have sneaked a bite after we'd all left (maybe *that's* what Sam had been shouting—not aliens at all) and . . . and . . . had an allergic reaction to one of the fillings. Or maybe it had given her food poisoning? Yes! That must have been it.

"Don't worry. I know what the problem is," I told her. "You had a slice of Sam's sandwich, didn't you? That's why you sent us all into Miss Patterson's class this morning, so no one would see."

Mrs. Ample shook her head.

"No? You mean it was *two* slices?"

More head shaking.

"Three?"

But Mrs. Ample kept on shaking her head and groaning.

"Are you saying you ate the WHOLE THING? *Sweaty spaghetti!* No wonder you're feeling poorly."

Mom kept saying how Cat was eating for two now that she was pregnant, but Mrs. Ample must have been eating for twenty. More than that, even . . . she must have been eating for *forty*!

I was just going to offer to fetch help when Mrs. Penford came tearing up the field to join us.

"The ambulance is coming!" she panted, looking like she'd just run a marathon. "They should be here any moment."

An ambulance? Gosh. It must have been a really *bad* case of food poisoning. Poor Mrs. Ample. I mean, I know she shouldn't have eaten the sandwich in the first place, but still.

Mrs. Penford put her arm round the groaning substitute teacher, wiping sweaty hair out of her face. "It's going to be okay," she puffed. "That's it, nice long breaths."

"Is there anything I can do to help?" I asked. "Should I fetch Sam and find out exactly what was in it? In case the paramedics want to know when they get here?"

Mrs. Penford looked surprised. I don't think she'd even noticed I was there. "Fetch who?" she said. "Actually, yes, if you could fetch your classmates, that would be good. Miss Patterson's got her hands full with Ella at the moment—something to do with a Dorothy victory dance, whatever that is, and a twisted ankle—so we're more short-staffed than ever. Round up everyone you can find and send them back to class. I'll get another teacher for you as soon as I can. You'll have to finish the treasure hunt another time."

What about Sam's sandwich? I wanted to ask. *Shall I let him know where it's gone?* But the expression on Mrs. Ample's face told me it wasn't a good time to bring it up. In fact, she looked like *she* might bring up Sam's sandwich at any moment.

Yuck, I thought (not for the first time that morning).

Yuck, yuckity-yuck.

Chapter 17

Monday, May 6, 10:15 a.m.

The classroom was in chaos, with everyone shouting at once.

"Goodbye, Mrs. Ample!" students yelled out the window. Some of the more adventurous among them had clambered onto their desks for a better view of the retreating ambulance. "Get well soon!" they screamed above the noisy wail of the siren.

Another group was crowded around the whiteboard, where Ravi was drawing life-sized diagrams of his alien invader.

"What about its teeth?" asked one of the onlookers, struggling to be heard above the general racket. "What were they like? Black or purple?"

Ravi thought for a moment. "I didn't really stop to see. I was in such a hurry to warn Sam about his sandwich. But they must have been pretty sharp." He added some blood-smeared razor-sharp fangs in red marker. "I mean, they were strong enough to get through all those layers of bread in one bite—I reckon they could chomp off a leg or two if they wanted."

"Wait a minute. That's what Shaniqua said about the escaped tiger," piped up someone else. "She said he chewed through Mr. Hargrove's leg *and* the sandwich."

"*And* he attacked Mrs. Ample," added Shaniqua, pausing in her dramatic reconstruction (using the stuffed alligator head in place of a hungry cat) in order to set the record straight. "That's why they had to rush her off to the hospital so fast."

"Mateo said it's because she had sandwich poisoning," argued another voice. "He said she was the one who took it."

"Well, Mateo's wrong," said Shaniqua. "It was the tiger. *That's* who stole Sam's sandwich."

"No, it wasn't," said Ravi, adding a third head to his creature for good measure. It looked even more terrifying now. "It was the alien. I saw it with my own eyes."

"You're all wrong," Deena cut in. "It was Toby Fishwick. He stole the sandwich to mess with Sam's audition. That's what the police are doing here."

"The police are here? Oh, thank goodness," said Shaniqua. "They must have come for the tiger. I've been trying to think of a big cat catching plan all morning, but it's not as easy as you'd think."

Ravi shook his head. "It's more likely someone reported strange flashing lights coming from the school. But the police won't be able to do much. They don't have alien clearance. They'll have to wait for the Anti-Extra-Terrestrial Task Force to arrive."

"For the last time, it wasn't an alien who took Sam's sandwich," said Shaniqua. "It was the tiger."

"No, it wasn't. It was Toby," Deena insisted.

"Mrs. Ample, you mean," said Mateo.

"Aliens," said Ravi, refusing to budge.

And then they were all shouting at once:

"TIGER! TOBY! TEACHER! CREATURE!

TIGER! TOBY! TEACHER! CREATURE!

TIGER! TOBY! TEACHER—"

"What's going on in here?" came a loud roar from the classroom doorway. It wasn't a tiger roar this time, though. It wasn't an alien roar, either. And it wasn't a sandwich-poisoned roar of pain. It was the roar of a teacher . . . an angry teacher.

"I *SAID*, WHAT'S GOING ON IN HERE?" The students stopped arguing. They stopped running around the room with alligator heads. They stopped waving out the window.

Shaniqua was the first to speak. "Mr. Hargrove!" she cried, running over to meet him. "Your leg! It's okay. It's still attached to the rest of you."

Deena wasn't far behind. "Oh, Mr. Hargrove, I've done something really bad. I'm so sorry. I did try to tell Mr. Lendworthy, only . . ." She burst into tears, leaving Mr. Hargrove looking from one to the other in confusion.

"Don't cry, Deena," he said, back to his usual calm self. "Whatever it is you've done, it can't be as bad as all that."

"It is," she told him through her sobs. "I borrowed a reference book over the weekend even though I know it's not supposed to leave the library, and I didn't bring it back this morning. Ella said she wouldn't tell anyone if I let her play Dorothy but I can't keep it to myself any longer. I thought that's what the cops were here for. I thought they'd come to arrest me."

Mr. Hargrove laughed. "The cops? You mean the traffic police who've come to give the fourth graders a talk on road safety?"

"Ohhhhh." Deena sniffed. "So they haven't come for Toby, either? But I heard him plotting in the bathroom. He was planning to steal Sam's sandwich to put him off his audition: *It's the perfect plan*, he said. *He'll be so upset when he realizes it's gone, that he won't be able to perform, and victory will be mine, all mine.*" She imitated the evil cackle.

Mr. Hargrove laughed even harder. "Hmm. It sounds like you overheard Toby practicing his audition piece. Unless I'm very much mistaken, that's one of the scenes from *Guitar Rivals II*. And as for this business with Ella, I'm not sure she's going to be doing *any* auditioning today. Or turning you into the librarian. I just saw her heading home with her mother and a very swollen ankle. I'll tell you what, how about I go with you at lunchtime and we'll explain everything to Mr. Lendworthy together?"

"Oh, thank you," said Deena. "That would be great."

"You see," cut in Ravi. "I *told* you it was the alien who took it. Not Toby. It was right here in the classroom," he explained to

Mr. Hargrove. "I saw its two heads silhouetted against the door and a strange flickering light."

Mr. Hargrove seemed to find that even funnier. "I think it was Mrs. Ample and the technician you saw, testing the projection equipment for your classmates' film projects. But I can see how it might have looked."

"What?" Ravi grinned. "You mean Mrs. Ample was the alien all along? Good thing I didn't karate-chop her into pieces, then!"

"Mrs. Ample's gone, Mr. Hargrove," said Mateo. "She ate Sam's sandwich and was so sick they carted her off to the hospital."

"Wrong again, I'm afraid," said Mr. Hargrove. "Mrs. Penford filled me in just now. It looks like her baby's coming earlier than expected. That's why Mrs. Ample went to the hospital. *Nothing* to do with a sandwich."

"Exactly. The tiger took the sandwich," said Shaniqua. "That's what I've been trying to tell you all. I thought he got you too, Mr. Hargrove. I saw the giant footprints in your garden and the chewed sneaker. And then I heard Mrs. Penford on the phone saying he'd eaten your whole leg."

Mr. Hargrove was laughing so hard now there were tears running down his cheeks. "Oh, Shaniqua! I've been looking after my sister's dog while she's out of town. *That's* whose paw prints they were. He chewed through my sneaker and then stole an entire leg of lamb off the counter where it was defrosting. It made him pretty sick, poor thing. I've been at the vet with him all morning. Why on earth would you think it was a tiger?"

"Because of the news report about the escaped zoo animal. They said it was a tiger." Shaniqua stopped and thought for a moment. "A ti-something, anyway. What else could it be?"

Mr. Hargrove dabbed his eyes with his handkerchief. "Well, the report I heard said it was a *ti*-ny little meerkat who'd escaped. But he's back safe and sound now, and as far as I know, he hasn't stolen any sandwiches."

"So what was the roaring sound coming from the school kitchen?" asked Shaniqua.

"The blender, perhaps? I asked the cook to make some celebratory milkshakes as a reward for all your hard work. I'm guessing that's what you heard."

"Thank goodness for that," said Shaniqua.

"What a relief," agreed Mateo.

"No invasion. Phew!" said Ravi.

"And there wasn't an evil plot after all." Deena looked much happier after her confession. "Mystery solved."

"No, it's not," said Sam, who'd been anxiously listening to the students' crazy theories. "The mystery's more mysterious than ever! If it wasn't an alien or a tiger or Toby or a substitute teacher who took my project, where's it gone?" *He* was the one roaring now. "WHERE'S MY SANDWICH???"

"Excuse me, Mr. Hargrove," came a cheerful cry from the hallway. "Milkshakes, coming through."

Mr. Hargrove stepped out of the way as the school cook came into the room, wheeling a cart of milkshakes . . . along with another cart behind that, boasting an enormous platter of sliced sandwich.

"Here we go," said the cook. "I saw Mrs. Ample put a sandwich in the fridge—I'm guessing it goes with the shakes? I've chopped it up to save you the trouble."

"My sandwich!" cried Sam, torn between happiness at finding it and shock at seeing it in pieces.

"Ah," said Mr. Hargrove. "I think I know what's happened here. Mrs. Ample must have taken it to the kitchen for safekeeping until this afternoon. She must have been worried about it getting hot if it was left out too long."

"And now it's ruined," sighed Sam. "I can't submit it to the fair like that."

"Oh dear," said the cook. "That's my mistake. I did take a photo of it on my phone to show the other cooks before I chopped it up, if that's any help. I'd never seen such a fine-looking sandwich."

"Hmm." Mr. Hargrove thought for a moment. "What if we asked Mrs. Penford to get the photo enlarged for this afternoon? You could display that at the fair instead?"

"And we can all try some now and write reviews for you," added Mateo. "Then you can include them as well." He reached out and snatched a piece before anyone could object. "Mmmm. Thib ib yummy," he murmured happily through a bulging mouthful of bread. "I gib it ten out of ten!"

"Great idea!" cried the others, diving in for their very own piece of sandwich-making history.

"All right," said Sam, grinning at the looks of delight on their faces. "No point making a giant sandwich if you can't share it with your friends. And there's nothing like aliens and tigers and police chases to work up an appetite! Here's to the craziest Monday morning ever!"

"And here's to the best project we've ever tasted," cried Deena.

"The gggrrrrrrreastest sandwich ever," agreed Shaniqua, roaring like a tiger.

"The finest food in the galaxy," added Ravi. "Three cheers for Sam's sandwich!"

"Hip, hip, hooray!" everyone joined in.

"Hip, hip, hooray!

"Hip, hip . . . BURP!"

"Sorry," said Mateo. "That'll be the cabbage."

About the Author

Jennifer Moore is a British freelance writer and children's author. She studied English literature at Cambridge University followed by a Research Masters at the University of Strathclyde in Scotland. Her fiction and poetry have been widely published on both sides of the Atlantic, and she was the first-ever UK writer to win the Commonwealth Short Story Prize. She lives in a small Devon town on the edge of Dartmoor and is an active member of the Society of Children's Book Writers and Illustrators.

About the Illustrator

Courtney Huddleston lives in Houston, Texas, with his wife, two daughters, and two cats named Lilo and Stitch. When he's not in his home studio working, he can usually be found playing video games, drooling over the work of other artists, going on long walks, or playing pranks on the family. While he gets inspiration from everything around him, his favorite way to get inspired is through travel. Courtney has been to most of the states in the United States, and he has visited more than a dozen other countries. He is currently searching for less-expensive inspirations.

CAN YOU GUESS . . .

WHAT HAPPENED?

WHAT HAPPENED?
LAB MICE HEIST

by VERITY WEAVER

Hardcover ISBN: 978-1-63163-307-2
Paperback ISBN: 978-1-63163-308-9

WHAT HAPPENED?
MATH TEST MISCHIEF

by VERITY WEAVER

Hardcover ISBN: 978-1-63163-311-9
Paperback ISBN: 978-1-63163-312-6

WHAT HAPPENED?
SANDWICH SHENANIGANS

by VERITY WEAVER

Hardcover ISBN: 978-1-63163-315-7
Paperback ISBN: 978-1-63163-316-4

WHAT HAPPENED?
STAGE TWO HULLABALOO

by VERITY WEAVER

Hardcover ISBN: 978-1-63163-319-5
Paperback ISBN: 978-1-63163-320-1

AVAILABLE NOW!

[4]